THIS WALKER BOOK BELONGS TO:

_____

_____

_____

_____

For Mara with all our love
S. H. & H. C.

First published 1995 by Walker Books Ltd
87 Vauxhall Walk, London SE11 5HJ

This edition published 1997

2 4 6 8 10 9 7 5 3 1

Text © 1995 Sarah Hayes
Illustrations © 1995 Helen Craig

This book has been typeset in Bembo Educational.

Printed in Hong Kong

British Library Cataloguing in Publication Data
A catalogue record for this book is available
from the British Library.

ISBN 0-7445-4771-7

THIS IS THE
BEAR
AND THE
BAD LITTLE GIRL

WRITTEN BY

Sarah Hayes

ILLUSTRATED BY

Helen Craig

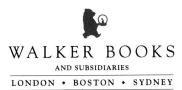

WALKER BOOKS
AND SUBSIDIARIES
LONDON • BOSTON • SYDNEY

This is the bear
who went out to eat.

This is the dog
who stayed in the street.

This is the girl
with the curly hair

who said she really
liked the bear.

This is the dog
who put out a paw

and tripped the woman
who came in the door …

... which pushed the people

waiting to pay ...

... and made the waiter
drop the tray.

This is the boy
all covered in cream

who went to the kitchen
to wash his face clean.

This is the girl
with the curly hair

who said, "You're coming
with me, bear."

This is the girl who
walked down the street

holding the bear
by one of his feet.

This is the dog
who thought it was fun

when the bad little girl
began to run.

This is the girl
who ran faster and faster

but this is the dog
who ran right past her.

This is the girl
who gave the bear back
and said he was
only a baggy old sack.

This is the boy
who said, "I don't care
if he's saggy or baggy,
he's still *my* bear."

MORE WALKER PAPERBACKS
For You to Enjoy

Also by Sarah Hayes and Helen Craig

THIS IS THE BEAR books

Three more rollicking cumulative rhymes about the adventures
of a boy, a dog and a bear.

"For those ready for their first story, there could be no better choice…
Helen Craig's pictures are just right." *The Independent*

0-7445-0969-6   *This Is the Bear*
0-7445-1304-9   *This Is the Bear and the Picnic Lunch*
0-7445-3147-0   *This Is the Bear and the Scary Night*
£4.50 each

MARY MARY

Included on the list of texts to be used in conjunction with the Standard
Assessment Tasks of the National Curriculum (Key Stage 2, Level 1 – 2)

"Giants are always popular with children and this fairy tale has a friendly giant
and an intrepid heroine, two excellent ingredients for a winning story."
Child Education

0-7445-2062-2   £4.99

CRUMBLING CASTLE

Three stories about the wizard Zebulum, his crow assistant Jason, and their
weird and wonderful friends.

"Gentle, cosy magic for solo readers at the lower end of the junior school who will
enjoy Helen Craig's amusing, detailed line drawings." *Books for Keeps*

0-7445-1726-5   £3.99